THE GIRAFFE WHO

COULDN'T GET A JOB

**Written by
Nick Stewart**

ISBN: 9798397534161

Earl the Giraffe liked lying on his bed, every single day.
Monday, Tuesday, Wednesday, Thursday, always till midday

He liked to eat and sleep and never ever clean. His roommate never visited, he found it all obscene.

Leroy liked to have a nap, once the house was clean.
He lay face first on his rug as part of his routine.

He dreamt about cleaning and working with a broom. Oh how much he'd like to be let loose to clean Earl's room.

One morning eating breakfast, Leroy had a word, "You're making my house such a mess, it's really quite obsurd."

Earl was surprised by this, he felt really hurt. "What can I do to help my friend? I'll stop dragging in the dirt."

Earl felt quite sad and he began to sob,
"If I want to stay here with my friend, I'll have to
get a job."

Earl knew what he had to do, but where would he start. The only thing he'd ever done, was teach himself to fart.

As Earl sat amongst his mess, he took a chance to read the Animal Express. He saw a job to be a cook so went along to take a look.

Earl went to the restaurant with a tie on to impress. He thought he looked really smart, like a gorilla in a dress.

The manager was friendly, but a bit over fed. He handed over a chef's hat, "put this on your head."

Earl put his hat on and started cooking dinner. It wasn't long before the manager called him 'a beginner'.

"I cant believe the mess you've made! Look at that fire! You're too messy and too unsafe, I don't think you're for hire ."

Earl left the restaurant and headed to the park. He knew he had to find a job before the sky got dark.

As Earl walked in rhythm, something caught his eye. "If your neck is long and you are strong please, can you apply?"

Earl entered slowly, hoping to do well. But, he hit his head, kicked the rug and oh no, he fell!

Earl left quite swiftly, the sky was nearly dark. "I'm so clumsy and so silly . . . I'll just go to the park."

Earl sat and pondered and his mind quickly wandered. "I can't do anything right, I guess I'm not that bright."

Out of the night appeared a panda. Black and white, her name, Amanda. "I'm big and round and shouldn't fly, but every night I touch the sky."

She told Earl to stop crying, never give up and keep on trying. "Everyone is good at something, especially a giraffe who's kind and loving".

Earl began running and started to reflect, "I should have more self-respect". "I am brave and I am tall, I could help others who are small".

And just like that he got his chance, he saw flashing lights pass at a glance. The firedogs went zooming by, "I could help them, at least I'll try."

The animals were shouting and one let out a yelp, "My ears are burning, my eyes are hurting, can anybody help!"

The firedogs got to work; Simon, Ruth, and even Kirk. Up the ladders they all went; it was quite a scary event.

as a hero, he'd rescued all the others. "Let's put our
[a]d to an end, you are brave and my best friend." Earl
and Leroy were friends once more, "Now let's go home and
clean your floor."

Earl had learned that everyone has a purpose. A giraffe from the jungle or a panda from the circus. We are all great at something, even if that is only one thing.

Illustrative Credits

Printed in Great Britain
by Amazon

31976837R00018